③

④

⑦

⑧

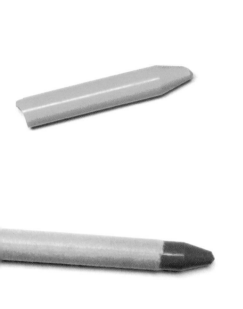

For
MOM

Henry Holt and Company, *Publishers since 1866*
Henry Holt® is a registered trademark of Macmillan Publishing Group, LLC
120 Broadway, New York, NY 10271 • mackids.com

Copyright © 2020 by Trenton McBeath
All rights reserved.

ISBN 978-1-250-18590-7
Library of Congress Control Number: 2019949494

Our books may be purchased in bulk for promotional, educational, or business use.
Please contact your local bookseller or the Macmillan Corporate and Premium Sales Department
at (800) 221-7945 ext. 5442 or by email at MacmillanSpecialMarkets@macmillan.com.

First edition, 2020 / Design by Sophie Erb
The artist used colored pencils, crayons, scissors, printer paper, various 19th-century oil paintings and etchings,
Popsicle sticks, pom-poms, glitter glue, sand from Coney Island, almond butter, strawberry preserves, Adobe
Photoshop, and a butter knife to create the illustrations in this book.
Printed in China by RR Donnelley Asia Printing Solutions Ltd.,
Dongguan City, Guangdong Province

1 3 5 7 9 10 8 6 4 2

RANDY,

the ~~Badly Drawn~~ Horse
BEAUTIFUL

T. L. McBeth

GODWINBOOKS

Henry Holt and Company   •   New York

Mom! Look!
I drew a beautiful horse!

He *is* beautiful!
Great job, dear!

I am a beautiful horse! Everyone loves me.

What's his name, honey?

I will call him . . .

Randy!

Randy must be the most refined and sophisticated name,
reserved only for the most special of creatures.

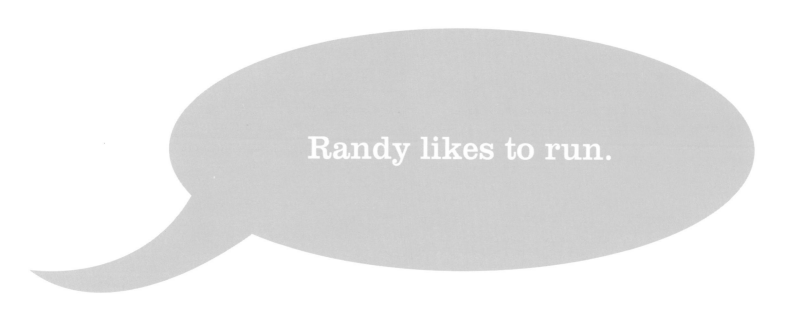

My gorgeous mane blows in the breeze.
My long, elegant legs glide across the ground.

My silky coat gleams and sparkles in the bright sunlight.
My perfect smile lights up the sky.

All that running made Randy hungry.

Ignore the squiggly lines and gurgly noises—
everything is fine with my stomach.

I am a great chef!
My culinary creations should be served at a five-star restaurant.

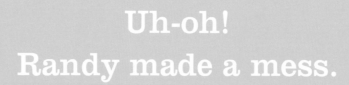

Uh-oh!
Randy made a mess.

Mmmm . . .

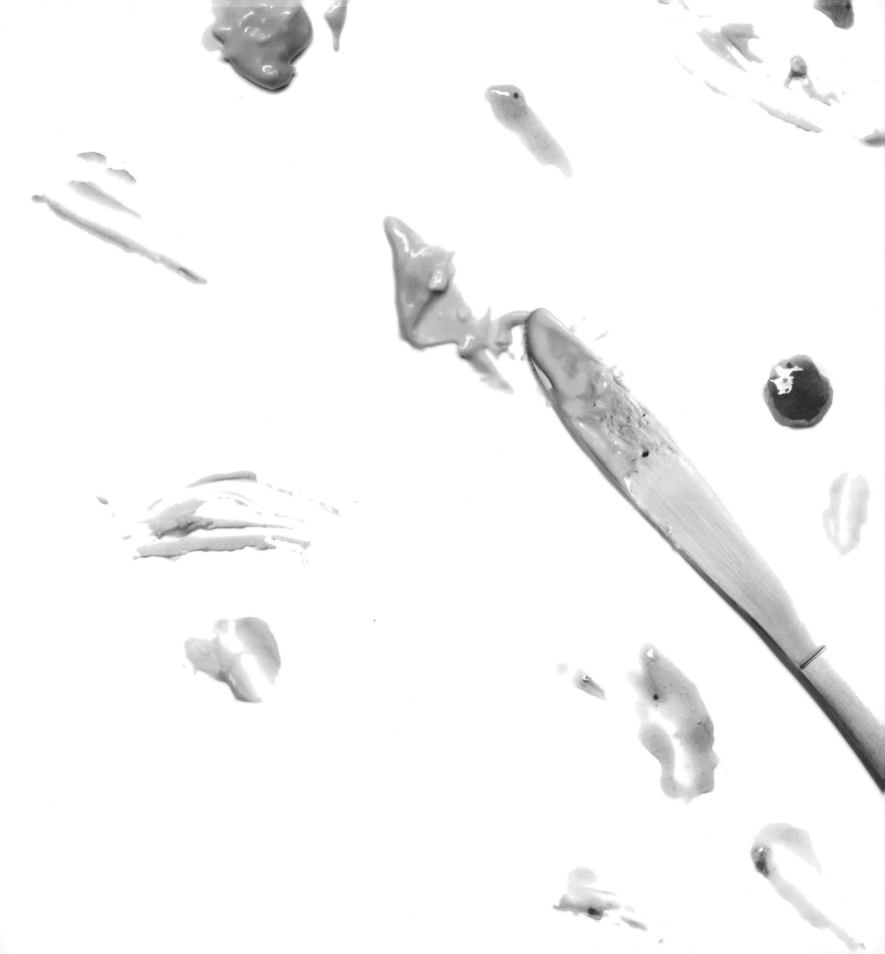

Randy cleans up.

Wait a second! I didn't make this mess.

But I suppose I could help you clean it up.

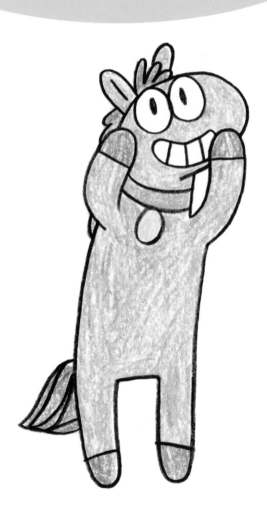

Now Randy is going to be a hero on an adventure!

This is more like it! A valiant quest of courage!

Surely I am destined for greatness!

He travels up a mountain.

But he gets stuck!

I'm okay! I'm not stuck . . . Everything is fine. Just one minute . . .
Who would put such a trap in the middle of a book?

I must press on. I am, after all, a hero
on a voyage to an unknown destination.

And the desert.

Sun is . . . so hot . . . So thirsty . . .

And going . . .

This is ridiculous! I've had just about enough of this adventure!

Randy finally arrives.

Phew! I need a drink!

Randy goes to the water to take a BIG drink.

Wait a second . . . Who is that? Is that me? I'm not beautiful at all! Where is my gorgeous mane? Where are my long, elegant legs?

My coat isn't silky or gleaming, and it's certainly not sparkly.
My smile doesn't even light up the sky!

All this time, I thought I was a majestic and beautiful horse!
How can this be?

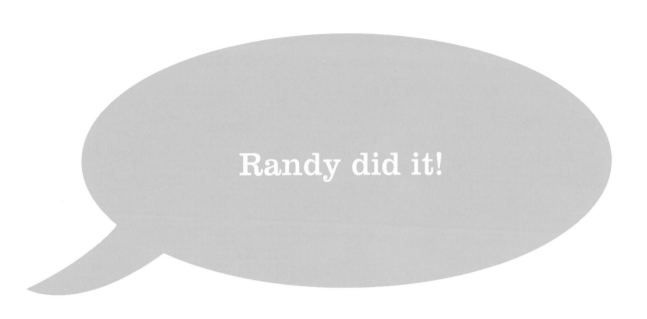

Did what?

He is a good adventurer!

Wait . . . I am?

I love Randy, my beautiful horse.

You do?

I am beautiful, aren't I?

HOW TO DRAW A HORSE
An in-depth and comprehensive guide